FLYING FERGUS

The Great
Cycle Challenge

FLYING FERGUS

The Great Cycle Challenge

CHRIS HOY

with Joanna Nadin

Illustrations by Clare Elsom

Piccadilly
PRESS

First published in Great Britain in 2016 by
Piccadilly Press
80-81 Wimpole St, London W1G 9RE
www.piccadillypress.co.uk

Text and illustrations copyright © Sir Chris Hoy, 2016

A CIP catalogue record for this book is available from the British Library.

ISBN: 978–1–471–40522–8
also available as an ebook

7 9 10 8

Typeset in Berkeley Oldstyle
Printed and bound by Clays Ltd, St Ives Plc

Piccadilly Press is an imprint of Bonnier Zaffre,
a Bonnier Publishing company
www.bonnierpublishing.com

Meet Fergus
and his friends . . .

Chimp

Fergus

Grandpa Herc

Mum

Daisy

Jambo Patterson

Calamity Coogan

Minnie McLeod

Belinda Bruce

Wesley Wallace

Dermot Eggs

Choppy Wallace

Mikey McLeod

. . .and see where they live

Fergus's house

Daisy's house

Grandpa's junk shop

NAPIER STREET

Bandstand

Play park

CARNOUSTIE COMMON

Bruce's Biscuits

Prince Waldorf

Dimmock

Demelza

Hounds of Horribleness

Meet Princess Lily

and her friends. . .

Princess Lily

Unlucky Luke

Douglas

Turret of Terror

Stables

Entrance to dungeon

Cook's pantry

Hounds of Horribleness Kennels

THE CASTLE

THE ENCHANTED FOREST

From Hero to Zero

Fergus Hamilton was an ordinary nine-year-old boy. He liked monster films (but only from behind the sofa), marmalade sandwiches (but only on white bread), and his dog Chimp (but only when he wasn't stealing his sandwiches). He didn't like school uniform (but he wore it), tidying his room (but he did it), or the way his mum tried to kiss him sometimes at the school gates (but most times he let her).

Yes, he was ordinary in almost every way, except one. Because, for a small boy, Fergus Hamilton had an extraordinarily big imagination.

Some days he imagined Chimp was a specially trained bomb disposal dog who helped him scout out unexploded World War Two missiles, instead of sniffing for socks under the sofa, which was what he was doing right now.

Some days he imagined he was an intrepid explorer living in an ice cave in the Antarctic, instead of a schoolboy living in the flat above his grandpa's junk shop on Napier Street.

Some days he imagined his dad lived with them, instead of in Kilmarnock, which was where Mum said he was, or in King Woebegot's prison in a parallel universe called Nevermore, which was where Grandpa said he was, and where Fergus himself had ended up only a few weeks ago. All he'd done was spin the pedals on his new birthday bike backwards three times and WHAM BAM! Suddenly he was no longer on Carnoustie Common but in the middle of an enchanted forest being chased by the Knights of No Nonsense and the Hounds of Horribleness. That had definitely been weirder than anything Fergus had ever dreamed of before.

Or maybe not. Because today Fergus was imagining he was on the winning team in the Great Cycle Challenge, edging past his arch-nemesis Wesley Wallace in the final few seconds to take the trophy for Hercules' Hopefuls, as the crowd went wild and Steve "Spokes" Sullivan himself declared Fergus Hamilton to be the best boy cyclist in the whole wide world.

But if there was one thing Fergus knew for sure, that really *was* a dream, and a hopeless one at that.

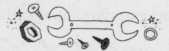

"If the wind changes you'll stay like that," said a voice from behind the *Evening News*.

"Huh?" asked Fergus, who had been absent-mindedly scratching Chimp, who was absent-mindedly chewing a shoe.

Grandpa lowered the sports pages and frowned at the boy. "Come on, sonny, you've got a face on you as long as the back straight. Why so glum?"

"You know why," protested Fergus. "Because the Great Cycle Challenge is in less than three weeks and so far not a single person has signed up for tomorrow's team tryouts."

"That's not true," said Grandpa. "Daisy put her name down the minute the poster went up."

"Daisy doesn't even have a bike," sighed Fergus. "And if she did her mum wouldn't let her ride it. She's not even allowed to play netball without a helmet."

"True," said Grandpa. "I bet the poor lassie has to wear that thing to eat her tea in case a pea pings off her fork."

"Or a tattie twangs her on the ear," said Mum, fastening her watch onto her nurse's uniform, ready for her night shift. "See you later, love," she added, kissing Fergus on the top of his head before he had time to duck.

"And be glad I don't make you wear gloves to hold your hot cocoa."

Normally Fergus would have grinned at that. But this evening not even the sight of Chimp trying to sniff out stray sausages in Grandpa's slippers could muster a smile. It was hopeless – his dreams of following in Spokes Sullivan's footsteps were disappearing faster than you could say "state-of-the-art suspension", which was something else he didn't have, his bike having been cobbled together from bits from Grandpa's junk shop.

"Och, I may as well give up now," he said, and flopped on the floor next to Chimp, who sighed in what seemed like sympathy, but was actually sadness at not finding any sausages. "It's impossible."

Grandpa put his paper down. "Now, that's not the Fergus I know," he said.

"What happened to the boy with the big dreams? The boy who believed he could take on all of Choppy Wallace's lot and beat them? The boy who believed that nothing was impossible?"

Fergus shrugged. "I don't know. But if you find him, maybe you could get *him* to sign up for tryouts."

"Look at it this way," said Grandpa. "A few weeks ago you didn't even have a big enough bike. Now you've got a great bike, a team name and the best coach in the business to boot, even if I do say so myself."

"But who are you going to coach?" asked Fergus. "The invisible man? The tooth fairy? Chimp?"

"Very funny, sonny," said Grandpa. "But I reckon tomorrow will bring some big surprises. And I don't mean your mam's broccoli and custard crumble."

Fergus felt the corners of his mouth twitch upwards. It was hard not to laugh at the time Mum had got the custard and cheese sauce muddled up.

And it was hard not to believe Grandpa when he was so full of fighting talk.

"Was that a smile, sonny?" Grandpa asked.

"Maybe," said Fergus, fighting the grin that was spreading across his face. But it was more than maybe. Because at last he had hope back in his heart – at getting a team together in time, and a good enough one to beat Wallace's Winners.

All of a sudden, tomorrow couldn't come quick enough.

Tryouts

The next morning Fergus lay in bed trying to focus on the two tasks ahead of him. He had to get back to Nevermore and find his dad, so he could get his whole family together again. And he had to turn himself into the next Spokes Sullivan, winning the Great Cycle Challenge, the city's biggest annual bike race, which wound through the old streets and across the bridges, hundreds of supporters lining the route to cheer the cyclists on and across the finish line. But as Fergus stared at the posters of Spokes he'd stuck up for inspiration, his dreams dissolved and his smile slipped.

He got a familiar sinking feeling – he'd been kidding himself, hadn't he? Grandpa's fighting talk was nothing but a bucketful of desperation. There was no way he could rescue his dad from a fantasy land he wasn't even entirely sure was real, and there was no way anyone was going to turn up for tryouts. Except maybe Wesley Wallace and his sidekick Dermot Eggs, and they would only laugh at him, Fergus Hamilton, the big loser that he was.

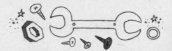

Fergus still hadn't cheered up by the time he, Grandpa and Daisy sat down on a bench on the common that afternoon.

"This is pointless," he said, checking his watch. Five to three. Five minutes to go and the only sign of anyone else in the area was Chimp, who was chasing a fly, and Mrs MacCafferty's cat Carol, who was chasing Chimp.

"Balderdash," said Grandpa. "Piffle," agreed Daisy. "Someone will show up. Just you wait and see."

Fergus glanced at his watch again. "Three minutes," he said, to no one in particular.

"I could always try out on your bike," suggested Daisy. "It's not like I don't know how to ride. I was Class Four Cycling Proficiency Champion until I fell off that time. I only grazed my knee but Mam went ballistic and banned bikes until kingdom come, which it never does."

"Och, Daisy, love," said Grandpa. "You know we'd have you on the team in a shot, but until you've got a bike of your own, and until your mammy says you can ride it, it's two feet for you, not two wheels."

"Anyway, you haven't ridden in ages," said Fergus. "And racing's not as easy as you think."

"Yeah?" Daisy raised an eyebrow. "You seem to manage it. Or maybe you're just scared I'll show you up. I did always used to beat you, after all."

"Once or twice," snapped Fergus. "And only because my bike was too small."

"Hey, hey," said Grandpa. "This isn't the time for falling out. If we're going to be a team we need to stick together, however hard-done-by we may feel at times.

"You're right," said Fergus.

"Sorry, Fergus," said Daisy. "But it's still SO unfair."

"We'll sort it one day, Dais," said Fergus. "I promise." He checked his watch. One minute to three. "But it looks like there's no team to join anyway." And he stood up ready to trudge home.

"Hold your horses, sonny," said Grandpa, peering into the distance towards the climbing frames. "That looks like a bike to me. But who, or what, is riding it?"

Fergus and Daisy turned to see a boy heading in their direction. Or what might have been a boy, only he appeared to be at least two feet taller than Fergus, and most of that was leg.

"Blimey," said Daisy.

"Crikey," agreed Fergus.

"Do you know him?" asked Grandpa. "Who is it?"

"That," sighed Fergus, "is Prescott Primary's walking disaster area."

"Not . . ." began Grandpa.

"Yes . . ." said Daisy

"The one and only Calamity Coogan?"

"Yup," sighed Daisy and Fergus together. "The very same."

Calamity Coogan wasn't the only one heading their way. From the other side of the common a tiny figure with curly bunches and a pink helmet was riding a titchy bike towards them.

"Minnie McLeod," said Fergus. "Seriously? But she's only seven. And she's . . . she's . . ."

"You'd better not be about to say 'she's a girl', Fergus Hamilton, or you'll have me to answer to." Daisy stuck her hands on her hips and fixed him with her killer stare. "Besides, she's Mikey's little sister and he's the number two racer on Wallace's Winners."

Fergus turned to look at Mikey, who stood over by the toilets scowling, his hands stuck in his pockets. It seemed like he'd rather be anywhere else than looking after his little sister.

And little was the right word, thought Fergus. That was the problem. "I wasn't going to say 'girl'," he replied quickly. "I was just going to say that she's, well, a bit . . ."

"Small?" asked Minnie, who had somehow managed to sneak up behind them in record time.

"Er . . ." began Fergus, his cheeks

flushing with embarrassment.

Minnie smiled. "It's okay," she said. "I know I am. But just because I'm little doesn't mean I can't do big things."

"Never a truer word spoken," said Grandpa. "Welcome, Minnie, and . . . Calamity, is it?"

The tall, gangly boy nodded as he hopped off his bike and came forward to shake Grandpa's hand. "Aye. It's Callum, really. But everyone calls me Calamity." As if to prove why, straight away he tripped over his own shoelace and went flying into a bush, sending Chimp, who'd been digging for treats or buried treasure, barking out in terror.

"Sorry," sighed Calamity, picking himself up. "These things just have a habit of happening to me."

"Never you mind," said Grandpa. "You just need to keep your kit in check, that's all. Besides, it's not what you're like on your feet that matters, it's what you can do with wheels. So, what say we find out, both of you?"

Minnie and Calamity nodded enthusiastically and settled into their saddles.

Daisy pulled a starting flag – a slightly grubby handkerchief – out of her pocket.

Fergus stuck his hands sulkily in his. He knew what Grandpa said was true: that a team had to believe in each other. But trying to believe in a walking stick insect and someone whose bike was so titchy it looked like something Chimp might ride was proving pretty hard.

"Okay, kids," said Grandpa as they lined up next to the bench. "To the

21

bandstand and back, let's see what you're made of."

"On your marks!" yelled Daisy. "Get set. GO!"

And they went, heading straight past the rubbish bins towards the bandstand.

"Well, would you look at that?" said Grandpa.

But Fergus wasn't looking or listening. All he could hear was the voice in his head. "You're a nobody, Fergus Hamilton," it was saying. "Always have been, always will be." *Wesley Wallace*, thought Fergus, glumly. *He's going to laugh me out of town when he finds out I couldn't even get a team together*.

But his thought was interrupted by Daisy. "Seriously, Fergus, LOOK!" she insisted, and yanked his head round towards the bandstand.

Fergus looked. Then he looked again

to be sure. But no, that graceful, swift cyclist really *was* Calamity Coogan. And that trickster doing a 180-degree turn on one wheel before zooming back towards him was none other than Minnie McLeod.

"Looks like we've found ourselves a couple of gems after all," said Grandpa as the pair arrived, barely out of breath, beside them.

"You were BEAST!" said Daisy.

"Brilliant!" admitted Fergus.

"See," said Minnie. "Little people *can* do big things." And she grinned.

"So are we on the team?" asked Calamity.

"You bet!" said Fergus. Then he clapped a hand over his mouth. "Aren't they, Grandpa?"

Grandpa laughed. "Of course they are. That was some incredible cycling, kids. Enough to give Wallace's Winners a run for their money."

"Not without a fourth member though," said Daisy. "It's the Great Cycle Challenge regulations. There's loads of them. You need four team members, all living in the city, and all under the age of eleven, and there can only be four teams maximum in the race. The winning team gets a trophy, their photo taken with the mayor, four tickets to the zoo, a hamper of cheese and biscuits . . . and a place in the District Championships."

"Crikey, did you memorise all that?" asked Calamity.

Daisy shrugged. "Who wouldn't? But where are we going to get a fourth team member in time?"

Fergus watched as Daisy bent to check Calamity's hydraulic brakes. Then he looked at Grandpa, who was busy fixing the saddle on Minnie's bike so she could get more height in her hops.

"Leave that to me," he said. "I've got an idea."

And, even if he said so himself, it was a right bobby dazzler.

Daisy's New Bike

"You, sonny, are a genius." Grandpa grinned over the kitchen table as he and Fergus surveyed their creation.

"Well, maybe a little bit," smiled Fergus proudly in reply.

And I am, he thought. Daisy might not have a bike, but Grandpa's junk shop had a whole fleet. Admittedly, most of them were in pieces, and a bit rusty, and hardly any had tyres. But between the bikes, and between the two of them,

Fergus and Grandpa had managed to build Daisy a brand-new second-hand cycle of her own.

"Now comes the hard part," said Grandpa. "Ready?"

"Ready," said Fergus.

Chimp wagged his tail. He was ready for anything that involved a walk, or better, a bike ride.

So, together, the three set off round the corner to Daisy's house.

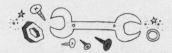

Daisy's house was as neat and tidy as Fergus's was chaotic. And Fergus knew that Daisy hated it. She hated the way she wasn't allowed to turn the sofa into a pretend castle in case she mussed up the cushions. She hated that she wasn't allowed to have a dog or a cat in case she turned out to be allergic or, worse, they got hairs on the sofa. And, most of all, she hated that she wasn't allowed to ride a bike anymore in case she fell off and grazed her knee again, or got mud on her trousers, or broke so much as a nail.

"Nothing is impossible," said Grandpa, as if he'd read Fergus's mind.

"Except Daisy's mum," muttered Fergus. "We must be doolally."

"Only one way to find out," said Grandpa, and pressed the doorbell.

The latch clicked open, and a pale woman peered nervously round the door. "Oh, it's you," she said, looking at Fergus's oily t-shirt and muddy shoes.

"It's all right, Mrs D," said Grandpa, "we won't come in. We just wanted to show Daisy something, and you too."

"Is that you, Fergie?" a voice hollered, quickly followed by legs bounding down the stairs two at a time.

"Oh, do be careful, Daisy!" wailed her mum. "You could trip and fall and break something."

"If you mean that old vase on the windowsill, I'm sure we'd survive," joked Daisy, flinging the door wide open. And that's when she saw it. "No WAY!"

"Yes way," said Fergus. "We made it for you. Well, Grandpa did," he added quickly.

"Aye, but you helped," added Grandpa. "Couldn't have done it without you."

But Daisy wasn't listening. "Are these old Velocipede handlebars?" she asked, touching the silver tubes in awe. "And check out the saddle! That has to be a Miller Classic."

"Aye," laughed Grandpa. "There's all sorts here. Velocipede, Miller, Criss-Cross – even some bits off an old washing machine."

"A w-w-washing machine?" stuttered Daisy's mum.

Grandpa nodded. "Just some old nuts and bolts. But don't worry, she's perfectly safe."

"Safe?" screeched Daisy's mum. "Safe? She could fall off. Or fly over the handlebars. Or . . . or . . . or get her trousers trapped in the spokes and be spun into smithereens!"

"Hardly," said Daisy. "I'd be wearing shorts."

"And a helmet, of course," said Grandpa.

"But –"

"Butts are for sitting on!" said Daisy. "PLEASE, Mum. I promise I'll be careful."

"I . . . I don't know," said Daisy's mum. "I'd need to ask your father in any case."

"Dad will say yes if you will," pleaded Daisy. "He doesn't go funny at the sight of blood like you do."

Daisy's mum turned paler than ever.

"But there won't BE any blood," said Fergus quickly.

"We'll take good care of her, Mrs D," added Grandpa. "I promise."

"Well . . ." began Daisy's mum.

"Please?" begged Daisy. "I promise I won't make a swamp in the bathtub again. I won't try to climb the drainpipe. And I'll never ever eat a chocolate that has been on the floor for more than five seconds."

"ANY seconds!" cried Daisy's mum.

"Deal!" yelled Daisy.

"But –"

"Butts are for sitting on!" chorused Fergus and Daisy, as they danced around the bike.

"You won't regret this, Mrs D," said Grandpa. "She's got what it takes, your Daisy. I know it."

"Can I have a go now?" begged Daisy. "Can I?"

"Not until you've got a helmet," said her mum. "And shin pads and elbow pads and an emergency first aid kit."

"Fine by me," grinned Daisy, who would have agreed to wearing a spacesuit if it meant she could ride a bike.

"So maybe tomorrow then?" asked Fergus hopefully. "Team practice in the park at four o'clock."

"Tomorrow," said Daisy happily.

Fergus smiled. Kingdom might never come, but tomorrow definitely did.

"I don't believe it," said Fergus as he and Grandpa trod back down Napier Street and climbed the stairs to the flat. "She actually said yes!"

"I knew we could convince her," said Grandpa. "The old Hamilton charm works wonders."

Chimp barked in merry agreement.

But it turned out Mrs Devlin wasn't the only one in need of some Hamilton charm.

"Fergus Horatio Hamilton and Hercules Jehoshaphat Hamilton, what in the name of all Caledonia have you done to my kitchen table?"

"Oops," said Fergus.

"Oh dear," said Grandpa.

"I'll give you 'oops' and 'oh dear'," said Mum, standing in front of what had once been a clean circle of pine with a vase of carnations on it, but now looked more like an explosion in a tool factory, with an oil slick thrown in for good measure.

"I can explain," said Fergus.

"You don't need to, Fergus," said Mum. "Grandpa was supposed to be in charge."

"Och, Jeanie," said Grandpa. "It was just to help wee Daisy out. I'll clear up now."

"And I'll help," offered Fergus. "We'll take everything back down to the junk shop pronto."

"That's another thing," said Mum, getting into her stride. "It's not just the mess up here. Downstairs is a complete catastrophe. And when was the last time you sold anything, Herc?"

"Um . . ."

But Mum didn't give Grandpa time to finish pondering. "I'll tell you. A year ago. And that was just an old bowl to Mrs MacCafferty for Carol."

Chimp whimpered at the cat's name.

"You need to have a sort out," Mum continued. "Or, better, sell the shop on."

"But . . . but that's your Hector's inheritance," said Grandpa. "And our Fergie's."

"Hector's gone," said Mum. "And Fergus needs new school shoes. And likely new trainers too."

"I'll do without," said Fergus. But he knew it was pointless. His trainers were already on the tight side. Another month and he'd be like the ugly sisters trying to squeeze on the glass slipper.

"We'll tidy up," said Grandpa. "And come up with a plan. I promise."

Mum nodded. "Thanks, boys," she

said. "Now I'm going for a wee wash-up and lie-down."

"Your mum's right," said Grandpa quietly, as soon as she'd shut the bathroom door. "It's time to sell up. I need to start bringing some money in now things are tight."

Fergus scrubbed a sponge up and down the table. "Maybe," he said.

"No maybe about it, son," said Grandpa. "It's time to man up and move on."

But maybe there was a maybe, Fergus thought to himself later that night as he lay in bed. Because what if Hector – Dad – wasn't gone after all? What if he could just get him back from Nevermore? Then everything would be okay, he knew it. But getting him back was going to be tricky. He'd disappeared in a parallel universe that was also home to a Swamp of Certain Death, a Well of Everlasting Torment and a mean king called Woebegot, who he hadn't met yet, but who sounded way scarier than any swamp or well, given that he'd banned cycling.

"We can do it though, Chimp, can't we?" he whispered. "Me and you."

Chimp stopped chewing a sock long enough to wag his tail.

"Yup, me and you, Chimp,' said Fergus. "The Dream Team."

And okay, so a sock-chewing mongrel wasn't as great a guard dog as a Hound of Horribleness, but Fergus was glad he had Chimp on his side.

Like Riding a Bike

"Don't worry about it," said Grandpa as he hauled Daisy to her feet.

"Everyone has to fall off at least once before they can call themselves a real rider," said Fergus.

"Forty-seven times, if you're me," shrugged Calamity Coogan, who was watching from the bank.

"It's all this padding," protested Daisy. "I feel like an Egyptian mummy."

"If it's making it more dangerous for

you then just take it off," said Fergus. "Your mam can't argue with that."

Daisy looked at Grandpa.

Grandpa shrugged. "He's right," he said. "A helmet, now *that's* essential, but otherwise, you don't need fancy kit, just good shoes with strong soles and clothing that won't get caught in the spokes."

That was all Daisy needed to hear. She quickly yanked off her elbow pads, shin pads, knee pads, shoulder pads and her massive padded anorak.

"Now just hop on and have another go," said Fergus.

But he didn't need to say it. Daisy was already back in the saddle and off again, sleek and quick this time, her legs pumping up and down like pistons. *She really is going to give me a run for my money*, thought Fergus, impressed.

"Hey, it's not just Daisy needs to practice," Grandpa said, as if reading Fergus's mind. "We've got less than three weeks until the Great Cycle Challenge and you all need some fine-tuning if you've a hope of beating Wallace's lot."

"In your dreams," said a voice.

Fergus knew who it belonged to. Only one boy was that mean, that often.

"Wesley," sighed Fergus, turning to see Wallace and his sidekick Dermot Eggs sat on the back of the bench, sniggering. "What are you looking at?" he asked.

"Losers," said Wesley. "That's what."

"Losers," echoed Dermot.

"Like you'll EVER beat us," continued Wesley. "With a beanstalk and two girls on the team."

"Yeah, girls," echoed Dermot.

"Just you watch it, Wallace," warned Daisy.

"Or what?" said Wesley. "You'll plait my hair for me?" He snorted. "Besides, every one of your bikes has got one wheel in the scrapyard."

"Haven't you got anything better to do?" asked Grandpa.

Wesley slipped off the bench. "Yeah," he said. "Might as well go and watch some paint dry. Got to be more interesting than this, right, Dermot?"

Dermot nodded. "Yeah, paint," he said.

"Dimwit," muttered Fergus as Wesley slunk off, Dermot loping behind him.

"Ignore them, all of you," said Grandpa.

"He's right, though," said Fergus. "They've been practising together for months and they've ALL got Sullivan Swifts. What chance have we got against that?"

"Every chance," said Grandpa.

"He's right," said Minnie. "I'm just as fast as my brother, whatever he reckons."

"And I will be," said Calamity. "Well, as soon as I can master the speed start. And stop," he added. "And everything in between."

"You lot are going to be the best," added Grandpa. "Fancy bikes don't matter half as much as brilliant riders."

"Too right," said Calamity. "Besides, 'Winner' is my middle name."

"Really?" asked Fergus. "Callum Winner Coogan?"

"Well, no," admitted Calamity. "It's Dave, but you know what I mean."

Fergus did. He knew what they all meant. They were a team. If they worked hard enough and long enough, then they might – just might – have a chance of wiping that smirk right off Wesley's face. So they'd better get to work.

And work they did. With Fergus taking the lead, the foursome got quicker and quicker.

"Stay in my slipstream, Daisy," yelled Fergus. "It'll save you –"

"Energy," finished Daisy. "I know. Twenty-five per cent. I read ALL about it."

"Then I shouldn't have to tell you to keep your elbows in," joked Grandpa, "seeing as you know it all."

"Ooops!" said Daisy, pulling her arms in tight and lowering her body over the handlebars, just like Fergus, Minnie and Calamity. "Wow! That feels brilliant!"

Fergus smiled as he glanced back at her. He knew that feeling well: your body and bike surging forward, as if they were one. Like you were about to take off. Like you were about to fly . . .

And that's when it came to Fergus. He and Grandpa had got the team sorted, so he could get on with the other job at hand: getting his dad back from Nevermore. And what better time than right now?

He pulled up and let the others pass him.

"What's up?" asked Grandpa. "Don't tell me you've run out of steam."

"No," said Fergus, which was true. "I just . . . I just need a wee." Which wasn't.

"Okay, sonny. Be quick, mind. I want to play Devil Take the Hindmost in a mo, set up the rankings."

Fergus nodded, remembering the racing game where the last rider round got knocked out each time. "I'll be back in five minutes," he said. "Promise."

As he headed off towards the toilets, Fergus knew he would be back in five minutes. Less, if it all went to plan. Because however long Fergus spent in Nevermore, he'd return to this world at the exact same second he'd left it. At least, that was what had happened last time. He just hoped time didn't work in the same way in Nevermore or he'd be heading straight for a chase with the Hounds of Horribleness.

Fingers crossed I get lucky, he thought to himself as he rounded the hut, out of sight of the gang. I just need to . . . be brave? He thought about what Grandpa would say right now. That was it! "I need to keep my eyes on the prize."

And what bigger prize could there be than to get his dad home? With that thought firmly in his head, Fergus pushed down hard on the pedals.

One-two, one-two. He felt the air rush past him, saw the grass and bushes blur into a wash of green. He felt his legs ache with the pace, and his heart race as he realised with a surge of joy that he was almost there.

Fergus shut his eyes, let his feet stop pumping, and felt the pedals spin the other way.

Once, twice, three times . . .

Unlucky Luke

WHOMP! Fergus hit the ground hard, but this time he'd known to bend his legs to absorb the impact – all those bunny hops he'd been practising had helped – and managed to pull up before hitting what looked like – yes it was – a purple tree.

"You've done it, mate."

Fergus looked down at the familiar figure cadging a lift on the crossbar. "Chimp?"

"That's my name," said the dog. "Don't wear it out."

"But you weren't even with me," Fergus pointed out. "How . . ."

"Don't ask me, mate. I'm a dog, not a flaming fortune-teller."

Before Fergus could even think about what that meant, he was interrupted by another voice.

"Chimp!"

"For the love of lamingtons," muttered the dog. "I said –"

Ignoring the dog's protestations, Fergus swung round to see a familiar figure running towards him, wearing an emerald gown with ruby buttons and a muddy hem.

"Princess Lily!" Fergus exclaimed. "You're safe!"

"Safe?" she said, puzzled.

NO CYCLING

Fergus looked nervously over his shoulder. "The last time I was here, the Hounds of Horribleness and the Knights of No Nonsense were chasing you – I mean us." He felt a shiver run from the top of his scalp all the way down to his toes.

"Oh, that," said Lily matter-of-factly. "They'll all be back at the palace by now. Getting them off my trail was easy-peasy. I just hid out at my friend's house before heading back here to wait for you."

"Your friend?" asked Fergus, before catching sight of an utterly unfamiliar figure approaching from the edge of the clearing. It was a boy, pale and tall and gangly with what looked very much like . . . chicken claws, attached to scaly yellow chicken legs.

"Fergus, meet my good friend," said Princess Lily. "Unlucky Luke."

"Unlucky Luke?" asked Fergus again.

"By name and by nature," sighed Luke, holding out his hand.

Fergus took it and shook it, but found it hard to keep his eyes off the scaly ankles and sharp talons.

"It's a long story," said Luke.

"So what's the short version?" asked Chimp.

"His dad's the palace magician," said Lily. "Percy the Prestidigiwotsit."

"Prestidigitator," said Luke. "It means magician."

"Only he's been Percy the Pretty Useless ever since he forgot the formula for the potion to turn people into animals," said Lily.

"And turn them back again," added Luke, pointing to what should have been his feet.

"But that's another story for another day," announced Lily. "Because right now, what we need to be focusing on is *you* giving *me* a go on your Hamilton Herc!" And she patted the handlebars of Fergus's bike as if it were a favourite pony.

"Well . . ." began Fergus, thinking

that wasn't really why he'd come here.

"Not a great idea," said Chimp. "Have you ridden a bike like this before? The crossbar is only the first of your worries. I mean, are you familiar with the fixed gear system?"

Lily shook her head. "I'm not familiar with any system," she admitted.

"None of us are," added Luke. "Given there haven't been any bikes in Nevermore since the cycling ban."

"Well, except in . . . *you know where*," whispered Lily.

"You know what now?" asked Chimp.

Lily leaned forward. "In the –"

"Don't say it!" interrupted Luke. "You never know who's listening. The trees might have ears."

Lily rolled her eyes. "Only if your dad's been messing about with them," she said.

Fergus, whose own ears had pricked up at the thought of anywhere secret where his dad might be hiding, found himself demanding an answer. "Where, Lily?" he urged.

Lily shot a look at Luke, who shrugged and then nodded, as if giving her permission to spill the beans. She turned back to Fergus and Chimp, who seemed as keen as his owner – or co-rider – to know what was going on. "There's this place to the north of the castle," she began. "I've never been, but I've seen glimpses from my turret."

"Glimpses of what?" demanded Fergus impatiently.

Lily took a deep breath, and checked around her, before whispering, "Dead things."

Chimp began shaking. "Dead what?"

he asked. "Dead dodos? Dead dragons? Dead . . . dogs?"

"No!" Lily exclaimed, patting him, before turning back to Fergus.

Fergus gasped. "You mean . . . ?"

Lily nodded. "A bicycle graveyard."

As Chimp breathed a sigh of relief, Fergus felt his tummy twitch and his thighs tremble. This was it! A lead! If the bikes were there, surely his dad would be nearby?

"It's the most terrifying place in the kingdom," continued Lily. "No one dares enter."

"Worse than the Well of Everlasting Torment," whispered Luke.

"Or the Dungeon of Despair," added Lily. "All those twisted corpses." She shuddered.

"And the ghosts," added Luke, trembling. "The King says the spirits of ancient cyclists haunt the land, hunting for children who dare to cross the boundary."

Never mind twisted corpses and ghouls, thought Fergus. He had to get to the graveyard, he just had to. But how could he persuade Lily and Luke. Unless . . .

"We could build you a bike," he blurted.

"Huh?" asked Lily, in a most unprincessy manner.

"That's it!" Fergus exclaimed, more sure of it now. If Grandpa had done it for Daisy, he could do it for Lily, couldn't he? "We'll build you a bike," he continued. "From the bits left over in the graveyard. There's bound to be enough."

"Do you . . . do you know how to do that?" asked Lily excitedly.

"Of course he does!" said Chimp. "My boy's as good with a spanner as he is in the saddle."

"So what do you think?" asked Fergus.

"What about the ghosts!" wailed Luke.

"Just a story," said Fergus quickly. That's what Grandpa said, anyway. And okay, so talking dogs and flying bikes weren't exactly everyday occurrences, but even Fergus thought some things were beyond the possible.

"Just a story?" Luke asked, sounding a bit less worried.

Fergus nodded.

Lily looked at him, then at Chimp, then back at him again. "Then I think yes!" she declared. "Yes with ice cream and a cherry on top!"

"Let's go!" said Fergus.

"To the bicycle graveyard!" cried Lily.

"The bicycle graveyard!" echoed Chimp and Fergus.

"The bicycle . . . graveyard," gulped Luke.

As the foursome set off through the woods, not even Luke's hesitation, or the memory of the Knights of No Nonsense and the Hounds of Horribleness could deter Fergus. They had a job to do, and he was pretty sure that, together, they could pull it off.

The Bicycle Graveyard

The bicycle graveyard wasn't hard to find, and it wasn't hard to sneak through the rusting railings either. But once they were inside, looking around was pretty tough. Surrounding them were the twisted bodies of bicycles: sleek racers with once-elegant wheels, fat-bodied BMXs and mountain bikes as rugged as the terrain they crossed. But now all were damaged, dusted with dirt and decay.

"It's . . ." began Fergus.

"Horrible," finished Lily for him.

"Atrocious," added Luke.

"Totally non-bonzer," agreed Chimp.

Fergus nodded. It was, it really was, seeing all those bikes broken and bent, instead of being ridden and enjoyed.

But he had to think of it a different way. Just like Grandpa had taught him, he had to turn it into a positive. That wasn't hard to do because here in front of him weren't just dead bikes but the frames and wheels and parts that would create new life – a bike for Princess Lily.

His eyes met Chimp's, and the pair nodded in understanding. "Let's get to work," he said.

So they did. With Chimp's bottomless pocket of tools, Fergus's deft fingers, Lily's yelps of encouragement and Luke's wise decision to stay on the sidelines, having already got his toes – or rather claws – trapped in a chain, they built a bike. It may not have been as shiny as a Sullivan Swift or as handsome as a Hamilton Herc, but it had two wheels and handlebars and a saddle that didn't have springs poking through the leather. As well as a stealth shield, smoke generator and bunny hopper, of course – no bike in Nevermore would be complete without those.

"I LOVE it!" declared Lily.

"Me too!" agreed Luke.

"You sure you don't want one, mate?" asked Chimp, twirling his spanner.

Luke looked down at his feet. "Not until I can get these sorted," he said sadly. "The claws would only get stuck in the pedals."

"Well, wellies won't," said Lily, looking at her own feet. "I'm going to take it for a spin right NOW!"

"Hang on . . . wellies?" asked Chimp, looking at her unlikely footwear.

"They're so I don't get my satin slippers messy from the swamp," sighed Lily. "Mum goes mad if I get dirty."

"Slippers would be better for cycling, but really you need some sneakers, kid," said Chimp. "And something less . . . girly?" He nodded at her enormous dress.

"Chimp!" warned Fergus. "What he means is, something that isn't going to get tangled in the wheels or turn into a parachute behind you."

"That's what I said!" said Chimp.

"Besides," said Fergus. "There's something I need to ask you before you go off anywhere."

"Anything!" blurted Lily. "I owe you one big cherry-topped favour, so ask away."

Fergus took a deep breath. He'd never said this out loud before, because he was worried if he did it would sound crazy, like the kind of thing you read in fairytales. But here, in the grounds of a castle, with a boy with chicken feet and a real-life princess (even if she was wearing wellies and a wonky crown) it suddenly seemed entirely possible. "Well, the thing is . . ." he began.

And he told her and Luke the whole story, or as much as he could. That his surname was Hamilton and his Grandpa was called Hercules, so it couldn't be a coincidence about the name of the bike. And that his dad had gone missing at the same time that the King of Nevermore banned cycling and banished the man who'd beaten him in the race. The man Fergus thought was his dad.

"It has to be!" said Lily. "It's him, I

know it! He's the man Dad banished!"

"Which is my next question," said Fergus. "Where?"

"The Turret of Terror?" wondered Luke.

"The Dungeon of Despair?" suggested Lily.

"Or the Pit of Permanent Pain," said another voice. "Where he'll have been eaten by the palace dragon. If he was lucky."

Fergus gulped. Even he knew that voice, and he'd only heard it once before. It was . . .

"Waldorf," said Lily. "I might have known you'd be spying on us. Oh, and look, you brought your pet monkey with you."

"Oi," said the thuggish boy standing next to the prince.

"That's Dimwit – I mean Dimmock," corrected Waldorf.

"Hard to tell the difference." Lily smiled. "Clearly."

Waldorf ignored his sister this time, his eyes flicking between the new bicycle and Fergus. "Well, well, well, we meet again," the prince said.

Fergus said nothing.

"Cat got your tongue?" laughed Waldorf. "Or maybe one of Pretty Useless Percy's spells has turned you as dumb as you look."

"Hey!" protested Chimp. "My boy's pure Hamilton genius."

"So I hear," said Waldorf. "Well, the Hamilton part anyway. And I'm sure King Woebegot would just *love* to hear all about that too. As well as all about the not one but TWO bikes you seem to have with you. Even if one of them does look like it's been taped together from an old pram and some scooter wheels."

"It so does not!" snapped Lily without thinking. "And Fergus didn't bring that one, he *made* it. For *me*. So *there*!"

"Even better," sneered Waldorf. "It's about time Daddy knew what kind of shenanigans you get up to."

"What about you?" demanded Lily. "You're always taking the hovermobiles without asking. And you don't eat your greens. And you never walk your dragon."

"Demelza? She's a bit . . . bitey," sighed Waldorf. "Besides, it's not my job to walk anything. That's what servants are for. Unless . . ."

"Unless what?" demanded Lily.

Waldorf smiled, the kind of smile a crocodile leers before it lunges. "Unless you walk her for me."

"Why would I do that?" said Lily, incredulous.

Waldorf smirked. "To buy my silence. If you don't, I'll go straight to Daddy with what I know."

Fergus looked pleadingly at Lily. He needed to stay secret if he was ever going to find and rescue his dad. And if he was going to get back to the park and the practice and the Great Cycle Challenge. He couldn't let the team down.

Lily gritted her teeth. "Fine," she said.

"Good," said Waldorf. "And of course you'll also be tidying my room for a month."

"What?"

"Including picking up all my socks."

Lily grimaced. But the worst was yet to come.

"And then there's the matter of finding a partner for the palace ball."

"I am NOT dancing with you. You're my brother!" exclaimed Lily. "More's the pity."

"Oh, not me," said Waldorf, absentmindedly brushing a fleck of dust off his pristine silver cape. "Him." And he nodded at his sidekick.

"Dimwit?" said Lily. "Never!"

"Shame," said Waldorf. "I'd better go and see Daddy this very minute, then." And he turned to go.

"Wait!" yelled Lily, to Fergus's relief. "I'll do it."

Waldorf didn't turn around again, just let his mouth stretch into a sneering grin. "Good," he said. "I'll expect you in five minutes for sock duty." And with that he stalked off, Dimmock lolloping behind him.

"Thank you!" said Fergus to Lily. "Now it's me who owes you."

"No you don't," said Lily. "We're friends, aren't we? Friends always stick together."

Fergus smiled. Of course they were. She may not be his best friend, like Daisy, but Princess Lily was coming close to second. She was feisty, she loved bikes, and she seemed to be able to read his mind too.

"But –" he began.

"I know what you're going to say." Lily's smile slipped into something more like sorrow. "We can't look for your dad. Not right now, anyway. Waldorf will be onto us."

Fergus nodded.

"But we will," Lily said, her face lit with belief again. "Soon. I don't care what Waldorf says – your dad's not in the pit, he never was. He's alive. I just know it."

"So when?" asked Fergus.

"Whenever you're ready," said Lily. "Give us a few hours to come up with a plan, and then pop back! Only not here. Too obvious."

"Come to my house," suggested Luke. "No one ever visits. Not unless they want to go away with green ears or a tail."

"How will I know it's yours?" asked Fergus. "How will I even get there? And when will I arrive? You could be waiting for me for ages." His head raced with time travel possibilities and strange logic.

Lily laughed, and even Luke managed a smile. "Oh, believe me," he said, "you'll know it's my house."

"As for when," said Lily, "I think it's kind of down to you anyway."

"What do you mean?" asked Fergus.

"Well, wherever you think about when you're flying, that's where you land. And when too."

"I'm in charge of time?" Fergus asked incredulously. "And space?"

Lily nodded. "Everything, pretty much."

"Then that's how . . ." He looked at Chimp. "I was wishing you were with me when I was back-pedalling."

"So Chimp appeared," said Lily. "Your imagination is more powerful than you know."

"Brilliant!" said Fergus, meaning it. Only this was more than brilliant, this was . . .

"Beast!" said Lily.

"Bonzer!" said Chimp.

"Now get going," said Lily. "The sooner you're gone, the sooner you can come back."

83

Fergus smiled and slipped onto his saddle. "See you soon," he said. Then he nodded at Lily's new bike. "And keep that hidden," he added.

"But I'll need to practise!" said Lily.

Fergus laughed. "Okay, well maybe use the invisibility button then."

"And try to get some new clothes," said Chimp.

"I will!" Lily grinned. "I know just where to go."

Fergus took one long look around him at the graveyard. He'd thought he would find his dad here, just hiding behind an old bicycle. But maybe, by telling Lily and Luke, he was a little closer to finding him. Life wasn't all about instant fixes – that's what Grandpa said. It was about patience and hard work. And he was a Hamilton, wasn't he? So he'd be able to manage both, in bucketfuls! Besides, there was the little matter of a cycle race at home to think about. That should take his mind off things at least. Just as long as he could get himself back to the park and to practice before Grandpa sent out a toilet search party.

But Fergus needn't have worried. No one had sent out a search party. No one had even noticed he'd nipped to the loo, because they were too busy celebrating Minnie's record lap of the bandstand and the fact that Calamity hadn't fallen off as he crossed the finishing line.

"We're going to do it!" cried Daisy. "We're not just Hercules' Hopefuls after all. We're Hercules' Heroes!"

"And heroines," added Fergus as he slipped next to his cheering grandpa.

Chimp barked in bewilderment, and Fergus cast an eye at his faithful, but now one hundred per cent doggy, friend. "And you, too," he said. "Whatever you are."

The Starting Line

Unfortunately, by the time the day dawned for the fiftieth annual Great Cycle Challenge, Fergus and his friends had lost some of their grit, half of their determination, and almost all of their hope.

"We've got about as much chance as a bunch of toddlers on tricycles," moaned Minnie, as she looked at the opposition.

Fergus followed her gaze. He had to admit she might be right. Not only were they up against Wallace's Winners, but the formidable Forth Fighters and the infamous City Slickers were on the starting line. Though he supposed he should be glad they'd even got this far. Daisy's mum had threatened to pull her out of the race when she found out it wasn't on nice soft, springy turf but two miles of not-at-all springy tarmac right through the centre of the busy city.

"You'll never get anywhere if you don't take a few risks in life," Grandpa had protested.

"I've never taken a single risk," snapped Mrs Devlin.

And look where that got you, thought Fergus. But he didn't say it out loud, just breathed a sigh of relief when Mrs D agreed that Daisy could carry on as long as she wore an extra pair of gloves and super-thick tights instead of shorts.

"I look like an eejit," protested Daisy.

"You look like a loser," sneered a voice from five bikes down. "Just like your number one."

Fergus's eyes fell on the wonky '1' his mum had hastily sewn onto an old jersey. He did. He looked like a loser. And he felt like one. His mum wasn't even going to bother coming to see him.

Of course she said she had to work a double shift, because they needed the money. But now Fergus wondered if it was because she just didn't believe he could do it. Which was fair, seeing as he didn't either.

"That's enough," said Grandpa. "I know what you're thinking and you're wrong. You've got as good a chance as any of that lot." He gestured at the rest of the front row. "So they've got brand new bikes and better jerseys. And, okay, the winner of the Under-Tens Individual Pursuit . . ."

Fergus flicked a glance to Minnie's big brother Mikey, who had the same steely concentration as her, but a lot more body, and leg power.

"But they don't have what we have . . ." Grandpa continued.

"Lucky socks?" suggested Minnie.

"Butterflies in their tummies?" tried Daisy.

"Scabby knees and a sore elbow?" said Calamity, who had tripped over his feet on his way to the fridge that morning.

"No," said Fergus, remembering what Grandpa had said. "Heart. We've got heart." And as Fergus said it out loud, suddenly he really believed it. Imagination was more powerful than anyone knew – that was what Princess Lily had said back in Nevermore – but so was heart, especially here, on this starting line.

"Aye, sonny," said Grandpa, smiling. "Heart. And hope. And they're worth more than a shelf full of trophies any day. At least in my book."

"Mine too," said Fergus.

"And mine," nodded Minnie.

"And mine," chorused Calamity and Daisy, grinning at each other.

"So what say we show them what we can do with those two things, eh?" said Grandpa.

Fergus smiled as his team nodded eagerly. "We will, Grandpa," he said. "We will."

But as the foursome settled into their saddles, and poised their toes on their pedals, Fergus couldn't help but let a drop of doubt slip down inside him again. This was the Great Cycle Challenge, after all. Spokes Sullivan had won it. Choppy Wallace had won it. Could he really join them in the ranks of champions?

There was only one way to find out.

The Great Cycle Challenge

"On your marks."

Fergus glanced round at his teammates as they shifted in their saddles, finding their centres of gravity.

"Get set."

He looked back and lowered himself over the handlebars. This was it. This was what he'd been waiting for: his chance to prove he had biking in his blood. Just like Grandpa. Just like his dad. So he had to do it – even if Mum wasn't here to see him, he had to do her proud. Fergus prepared himself for the starting whistle.

"Go!"

And they were off.

The team did exactly what they'd practiced in training. Calamity and Daisy were up front at first, letting Fergus and Minnie save their energy by staying in the slipstream. Only it wasn't as easy as it had seemed in the park. For a start, there were the crowds watching them, including James "Jambo" Patterson, the *News*'s sports reporter, whose cycling round-ups Fergus read religiously every Monday. Then there was the track, which, while it didn't have the lumps or bumps of the scrappy common, had new obstacles like potholes. And last but definitely not least there were the other teams. The City Slickers were neck-and-neck with Wallace's Winners, followed by Hercules's Heroes, and behind them were the Forth Fighters, who were using two back-up riders because their frontrunners, the Hegarty twins, had both got flu.

"Go on," Fergus urged Calamity in his head, as they rounded Princess Street into the second mile. "Make a break for it."

Somehow Calamity sensed Fergus's pleas and pushed harder on his pedals, Daisy following almost immediately. Fergus felt himself surge forward into the gap, with Minnie beside him.

"Go on, Fergus!" called someone in the crowd. But Fergus couldn't turn to see who. If he lost concentration for one second, he'd lose everything. *Eyes on the prize,* he told himself. And that prize was getting closer by the second. The City Slickers had fallen into third place now, and the gang were only metres behind Wesley's lot. They just had to find the power for a final push.

Calamity and Daisy knew what they needed to do and let up on the pedals for a split second, allowing Minnie and Fergus to fly forward and take the lead for their team. Fergus could feel his heart hammering in his chest, and the beginnings of cramp in his calves as his effort caused lactic acid to build up in his muscles.

"Ignore it," Fergus told himself. "It's just a twinge. Not far to go now."

And there wasn't. As the team turned onto the Fifth Bridge for the final straight, Fergus felt the pain subside. His pounding heart gave a leap of joy as he realized they could do it. They really could! Fergus was closing on Wesley Wallace – he could win.

Unfortunately someone else realised it at the exact same moment.

"Now," yelled Wesley, from his place at the front. And as he said it, Wallace's Winners all flicked their bikes to the right, sending Fergus and his friends into momentary chaos, before speeding off ahead of them towards the finishing line.

"Hold on!" Fergus called to them as he tried to right himself. "Hold steady!"

Minnie recovered as quickly as Fergus, but Calamity was teetering this way and that and Daisy was wobbling like a poorly set jelly.

"Come on," urged Fergus again. "We can still do it!"

But as the finishing line came into sight, and then disappeared behind them as they slowed to a squealing halt, Fergus knew he had been wrong. They hadn't done it. Not quite. And in the Great Cycle Challenge, not quite wasn't quite good enough.

Fergus climbed off his bike and let it drop to the ground, his own body sinking down after it. Minnie, Calamity and Daisy joined him, as they watched Wesley lead Wallace's Winners in celebration, spraying each other with soda water and holding the Challenge Cup high up in the air.

"Dirty cheats," said Daisy despondently. "They don't deserve their place."

"Och, never mind," said Grandpa, panting from pushing his way through the crowd and onto the track. "There's always next year. And we'll know what to expect from them then, and be ready for it."

"Next year?" said Fergus in despair. "Next year's . . . a year away. What are we going to do until then?"

"Practise harder," said Grandpa. "That's all it takes. Remember, talent's nothing if you don't work at it."

"I've got a better idea," said a Glaswegian accent.

Fergus looked up to see a face he recognised. Usually it was in black and white and stuck on the back page of

Grandpa's paper. But today it was right here in front of him, with a familiar smile and a quiff of dark hair.

"J-J-Jambo Patterson?" he stuttered.

"Nice to meet you," said Jambo. "Fergus, isn't it?"

Fergus nodded.

"Impressive performance out there," the reporter continued. "I thought to myself, *Finally here's a boy who can beat Wesley Wallace.*"

Fergus felt his heart sink again. "Not today," he said.

"True," said Jambo. "But there's always the Districts."

"What do you mean, Districts?" asked Daisy. "We just lost."

"No," corrected Jambo. "You came second. And this year the top *two* teams are going through."

"Seriously?" asked Fergus.

"Seriously," said Jambo. "I thought you knew. Fiftieth anniversary rules."

Fergus looked at Daisy who reddened. "I - I - I didn't memorise those," she stuttered.

But Fergus didn't care – all he could think about was that they were through.

"Brilliant!" he yelled, jumping to his feet.

"Yeah, beast!" cried Daisy, doing the same, her mistake forgotten.

"We're going to Districts!" the team chanted. "We're going to Districts."

The foursome spun in a circle, so quickly that Fergus didn't notice the arrival of the one person he needed to tell, until she was standing next to him.

"What did I miss, Fergie?"

Fergus broke away from the group. "Mum?" he gasped. "But how? When?"

"They let me off shift early," she laughed. "I came as quick as I could. Didn't you hear me shouting?"

Fergus nodded, realising. He'd wished for it, and it had happened, just like Princess Lily said it could.

"I take it you came first then?"

"No," said Fergus, still grinning. "Second. But we got through! We won anyway."

And as he felt his mum pull him into her arms, he knew that was the truth. He *had* won. Fergus Hamilton was a winner.

And so was Daisy, even though her mum had nearly fainted in fear watching her daughter wobbling.

And so was Calamity, who despite his name had managed to avoid disaster as long as he was in the saddle.

And so was Minnie, who had proved that a little can definitely go a long way.

But Grandpa Herc was the biggest winner of all, Fergus thought – he was their team coach, and the brains behind it all. If Fergus got his way, Grandpa would also be the brawn behind something else. Something he'd got the idea for back in Nevermore. And something Fergus really, really needed to tell Mum about before she took any more double shifts at the Infirmary.

Plan B

"A bike shop, you say?" asked Grandpa.

"You've got the shop bit already," explained Fergus. "And some of the bikes. You just need to get hold of a few more."

Grandpa nodded. "It could do repairs as well. And offer trade-ins on old models."

"And sell repair kits and spare tyres," reeled off Fergus, bursting with enthusiasm. "And even helmets and jerseys."

"What do you think, Jeanie?" Grandpa asked. "It is a winner?"

Fergus looked pleadingly at his mum. "It would mean no more night shifts. Well, not as many, anyway."

"And it'd keep the kitchen table clean," added Grandpa. "We can use the back of the shop for maintenance if I clear out the old dishwashers and dustbins."

"And –" began Fergus, trying to think up more reasons why she just had to say yes.

"No more ands, Fergus," interrupted Mum. "You don't need to convince me. You're right. It's a winner." She looked from her son to her father-in-law. "Just like both of you boys."

"It might take a while to get going," warned Grandpa. "And a lot of hard graft."

"But I'll help," piped up Fergus.

"We'll all help," said Mum. "You, me and Grandpa. The Dream Team."

Chimp barked as the fly he'd been chasing disappeared out of the window.

"And you, too," said Fergus, laughing at his dog. "You can . . . I don't know, be our mascot, maybe?"

"Chimp's Bikes?" suggested Mum.

"No," said Fergus. "I've already got a name. 'Herc's Hand-Me-Downs'," he announced.

"I like it," said Mum. "Make do and mend, that's what it means. And that's what lots of us have to do."

"Make the most of what you've got," said Grandpa.

"It's not all about brand new bikes," said Fergus. "Or being born a winner."

"It's about working at it," said Grandpa. "And we all do that, every day."

As he settled down under the covers that night, his blisters bandaged and his legs still aching just enough to remind him what he'd done that day, Fergus thought of Wesley Wallace at the finishing line, parading past with the cup thrust deliberately in his face. "You're a nobody, Hamilton," he had said. "A loser. Always have been, always will be."

At that moment, though, with Chimp snoring soundly beside him, and Mum and Grandpa downstairs drinking cups of cocoa and reading the *Evening News*, Fergus knew he was anything but. He may not have won the Great Cycle Challenge, and he may not have got his dad back from Nevermore – not yet anyway. But he had the best family in the whole world. Or Scotland, at least. And that was worth a hundred trophies.

Joanna Nadin is the author of more than fifty books for children and teenagers, including the bestselling Rachel Riley Diaries and the award-winning Penny Dreadful series. Amongst other accolades she has been nominated for the Carnegie Medal and shortlisted for the Roald Dahl Funny Prize, and is the winner of the Fantastic Book Award, Highland Book Award and the Surrey Book Award. Joanna has been a journalist and adviser to the Prime Minister, and now teaches creative writing at Bath Spa University. She lives in Bath and loves to ride her rickety bicycle, but doesn't manage to go very fast. And she never, ever back-pedals . . .

Sir Chris Hoy MBE, won his first Olympic gold medal in Athens 2004. Four years later in Beijing he became the first Briton since 1908 to win three gold medals in a single Olympic Games. In 2012, Chris won two gold medals at his home Olympics in London, and became Britain's most successful Olympian to date with six gold medals and one silver. Chris also won eleven World titles and two Commonwealth Games gold medals. In December 2008, Chris was voted BBC Sports Personality of the Year, and he received a Knighthood in the 2009 New Year Honours List. Sir Chris retired as a professional competitive cyclist in early 2013; he still rides almost daily. He lives in Manchester with his wife and son.

To discover more about Fergus and his friends join them at

FLYING FERGUS.com

There's loads to explore – learn more about Chris Hoy, watch videos and get tips and tricks for safe cycling and taking care of your bike. You can play games, solve puzzles and even get exclusive sneak peeks of new books in the series!

JOIN THE GANG!

Become a member of the fan club to keep up to date with Fergus, Daisy and Chimp and be a part of all their adventures. You'll have the chance to build your own Flying Fergus character and even choose your own bike to ride!